Angelina's Halloween

To my husband, Michael, with love   KH

To Sophie, as promised, with love   HC

PUFFIN BOOKS

Published by the Penguin Group
Penguin Books Ltd, 80 Strand, London WC2R 0RL, England
Penguin Putnam Inc., 375 Hudson Street, New York, New York 10014, USA
Penguin Books Australia Ltd, 250 Camberwell Road, Camberwell, Victoria 3124, Australia
Penguin Books Canada Ltd, 10 Alcorn Avenue, Toronto, Ontario, Canada M4V 3B2
Penguin Books India (P) Ltd, 11 Community Centre, Panchsheel Park, New Delhi – 110 017, India
Penguin Books (NZ) Ltd, Cnr Rosedale and Airborne Roads, Albany, Auckland, New Zealand
Penguin Books (South Africa) (Pty) Ltd, 24 Sturdee Avenue, Rosebank 2196, South Africa

Penguin Books Ltd, Registered Offices: 80 Strand, London WC2R 0RL, England

www.penguin.com

First published by Pleasant Company Publications 2000
Published in Puffin Books in hardback 2002
1 3 5 7 9 10 8 6 4 2
Published in Puffin Books in paperback 2002
1 3 5 7 9 10 8 6 4 2

Copyright © HIT Entertainment plc, 2000
Text copyright © Katharine Holabird, 2000
Illustrations copyright © Helen Craig Ltd, 2000
Angelina, Angelina Ballerina and the Dancing Angelina logo are trademarks of HIT Entertainment plc, Katharine Holabird and Helen Craig.
Angelina is registered in the UK, Japan and US Pat. & Tm. Off. The Dancing Angelina logo is registered in the UK.
All rights reserved.

The moral right of the author and illustrator has been asserted

Made and printed in Italy by Printer Trento Srl

Without limiting the rights under copyright reserved above, no part of this publication may be reproduced, stored in or introduced into a retrieval system,
or transmitted, in any form or by any means (electronic, mechanical, photocopying, recording or otherwise), without the prior written permission
of both the copyright owner and the above publisher of this book

British Library Cataloguing in Publication Data
A CIP catalogue record for this book is available from the British Library

ISBN 0–670–91162–3 Hardback
ISBN 0–14–056870–0 Paperback

To find out more about Angelina, visit her web site at **www.angelinaballerina.com**

Angelina's Halloween

Story by **Katharine Holabird** Illustrations by **Helen Craig**

PUFFIN BOOKS

Angelina loved the excitement of Halloween. She loved dressing up and trick-or-treating and spent hours with her best friend, Alice, thinking about wonderful costumes. At last they decided to be dancing fireflies and drew beautiful pictures of wings and tiaras.

Angelina's little sister, Polly, wanted to join them. "Look at this," she kept saying, showing them her funny scribbles.

Mrs Mouseling helped them make the delicate costumes,
and when the wings and tiaras were done, Angelina and
Alice practised flying around and around the cottage.

Polly tried to fly too but kept crashing into Angelina's wings.
"Why do you always copy me?" Angelina stamped her foot.

Polly hung her head. "I want wings," she cried.

"You're too little," explained Angelina, "but you could be
something really scary."

Mrs Mouseling found a sheet, and Angelina showed Polly
how to be a spooky Halloween ghost.

On Halloween evening, Angelina and her friends played scary games, and Mrs Mouseling made them a bubbling witches' brew and delicious goblin biscuits.

When Mr Mouseling came home with an enormous pumpkin, the two fireflies and the little ghost gave him quite a fright.

After the party, Angelina and her friends set off together with their trick-or-treat bags.

"Don't forget your sister," called Mrs Mouseling as the little ghost trundled after them.

They raced each other to the General Store and sang a song about spiders
and bats to Mrs Thimble, who had a great collection of Halloween
sweets. Then they went to scare Miss Lilly, the ballet teacher, who
waved her wand and gave them each a lollipop. They
were about to play a Halloween trick on old
Mrs Hodgepodge when all of a sudden …

..."BOO!"

Two red devils leaped out at them from behind an apple tree.
Angelina wasn't fooled and quickly recognized Spike and Sammy.
"We're not scared of you," she laughed.

"I'll bet you're scared of that house," teased Spike, pointing
up the lane. "It's haunted."

Angelina skipped off towards the dark building and
banged loudly on the door. "Trick or treat?"
she called. There was no answer.

"Let's go inside," whispered
Spike and Sammy.

Inside, the house was
strange and shadowy, and they tiptoed
around very slowly. "Ouch!" Alice stubbed her toe.
Angelina shivered, and then something lumpy bumped
into her. "Help!" she shrieked, and they all scrambled outside.

In the dark garden, a weird sound stopped them.
"OOOh. OOOh. OOOOoooooooh."

"Watch out for witches," Alice warned everyone.

They peered all around, and then Angelina saw a ghostly shape struggling in the blackberry bushes. "It's only Polly," she sighed, dragging the little ghost out of the prickles. "Now stay with me," she scolded.

After that, Angelina kept her eyes on the little ghost and they went trick-or-treating all through the neighbourhood, filling their bags with delicious sweets.

As the moon rose high in the night sky, the village band began to play and everyone came out to join the Grand Costume Parade.

The whole village was dressed up in marvellous costumes. The two fireflies seemed to float off the ground as they danced along, with the little ghost jumping beside them.

At the end of the
evening, Miss Lilly
proudly handed out prizes.
"The two fireflies and the
little ghost win a special award
for Halloween dancing," she announced.

"Hurray!" shouted the ghost, leaping up and down.

"But you're Henry!" gasped Angelina. "Where's Polly?"

Angelina dashed up the street to Mrs Thimble's General Store, but all the village shops were closed. She ran to Mrs Hodgepodge's cottage, but nobody was home.

Then a fuzzy monster skipped by. "Have you seen a little ghost?" Angelina asked, but the monster shook his head sadly.

Angelina raced up and down through all the streets of the village…

… until at last she reached the haunted house. There she found Polly, sitting on the steps, sharing the goodies from her trick-or-treat bag with three little friends dressed as wizards.

"My tummy feels funny," Polly whimpered.

Angelina shook her head. "You shouldn't eat your sweets so fast," she said. "Anyway, you really scared me."

"Did I?" Polly smiled.

On the way home, Polly held Angelina's hand.

"Next Halloween, can I be a firefly just like you?" she asked.

"Next Halloween, I think I'll be an acrobat," said Angelina.

"Can I…" Polly began, "…be an acrobat too?"

"First I'll have to show you some of my tricks." Angelina smiled.

And the very next day, she did.